TINY SNAIL

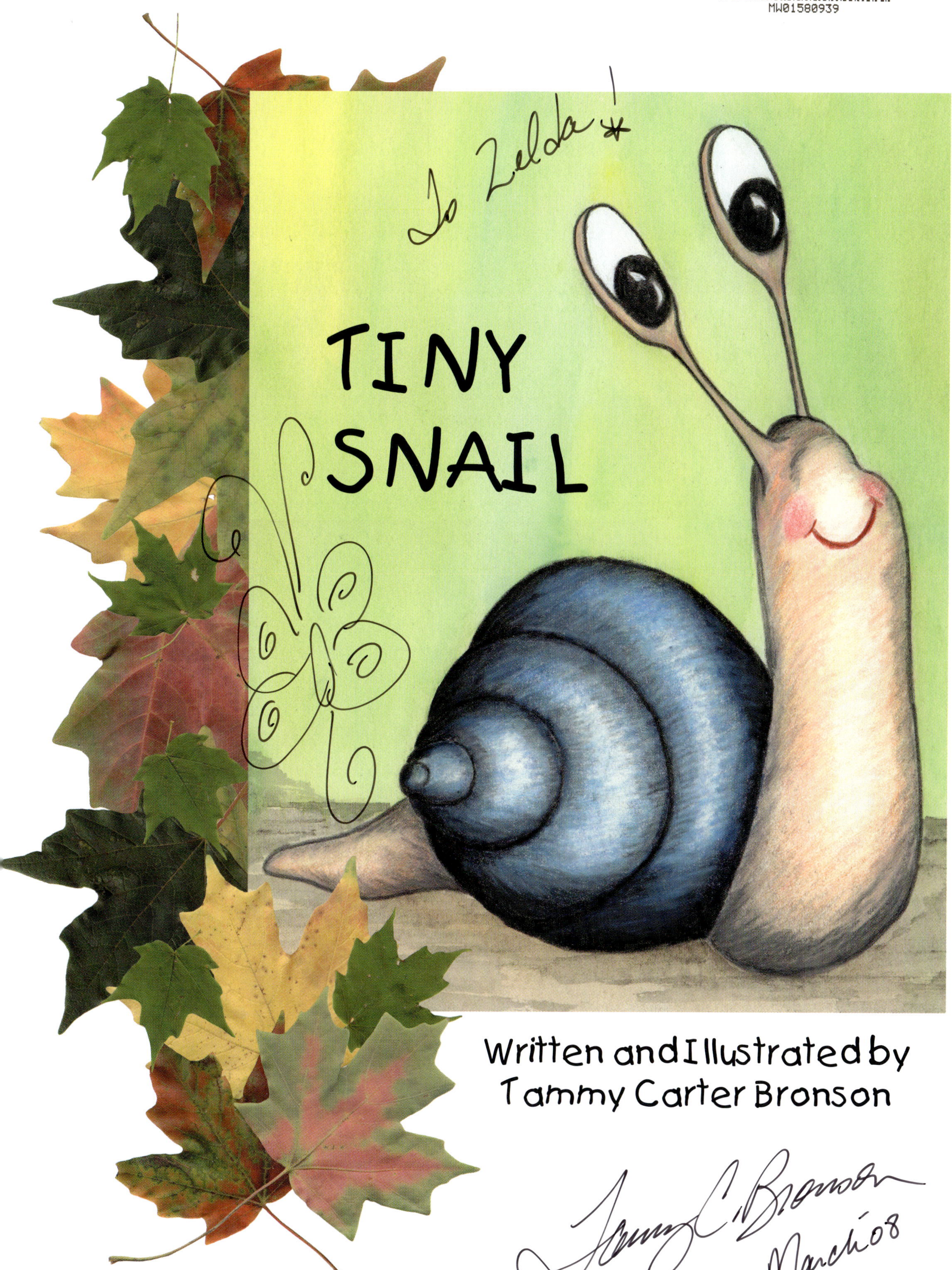

To Zelda!

Written and Illustrated by
Tammy Carter Bronson

Bookaroos® Publishing, Inc.
P. O. Box 8518
Fayetteville, Arkansas 72703 USA
www.bookaroos.com
books@bookaroos.com

Copyright © 2000 by Tammy Carter Bronson.
All rights reserved.

Bookaroos is a registered trademark
of Bookaroos® Publishing, Inc.
All rights reserved.

First printing 2000
Second printing 2002, Revised
Third printing 2002
Fourth printing 2005
Fifth printing 2005
Sixth printing 2007
Seventh printing 2007

Printed in the United States of America.

Publisher's Cataloging-in-Publication

Bronson, Tammy Carter.
  Tiny Snail / text and illustrations by
Tammy Carter Bronson.
   p. cm.
   SUMMARY: Tiny wants to live under the Maple Tree, but she cannot reach it in one night. Armed only with her friends' advice, Tiny crawls into a land with no shade. She battles sun, rain and mud, but Tiny always says thank you. When Tiny finally reaches the tree, she attains more than her goal: she learns to say thank you to herself.
   LCCN: 00-190287
   ISBN 13: 978-0-9678167-1-5, Hardcover
   ISBN 13: 978-0-9678167-2-2, Softcover
   1. Snails--Juvenile fiction. I. Title.

PZ7.B7893Tin2000   [E]
                           QBI00-901026

For
anyone
with a dream.

A very small snail lived deep in the forest. Her name was Tiny Snail. Her friends called her Tiny. One morning, Tiny could not sleep. Mr. Squirrel stopped by.

"What's wrong, Tiny?" he asked.

Tiny gazed at the Maple Tree standing alone on top of the grassy hill. "I want to live under that tree, but it's too far to crawl."

"Try," Mr. Squirrel said. "You can do it!" Mr. Squirrel scampered away.

Tiny slept during the day and dreamed about the Maple Tree. When evening arrived, her journey began.

She crawled

and crawled

and crawled.

The sun began to rise.

The tree was still far away when Tiny Snail fell asleep.

Tiny woke up. Her skin was tingling.

"Help!" she cried. Tiny Snail crawled toward the shade.

A shadow flickered on the ground. It was Miss Butterfly.

"I have to sleep in the shade," Tiny huffed, "or else the sunlight will dry out my moist skin."

Miss Butterfly balanced on Tiny's shell. "My wings will give you shade," she said.

When Tiny reached the shadows, she slumped inside her shell. "How will I reach the Maple Tree now?"

"Ask it to come closer," Miss Butterfly called as she toppled away on a current of air.

"Please, Maple Tree, come closer for I cannot crawl any farther," Tiny said.

Mother Turtle wobbled by. "What are you waiting for?" she asked.

"For the tree to come closer," Tiny said.

Mother Turtle laughed. "It won't come closer unless you crawl out to meet it."

"But it's too far."

"You can do it," the old turtle smiled. "Go a shorter distance first." Mother Turtle wobbled away.

Tiny looked at the hill and spotted a clump of dandelions.

"Oh, Dandelions! I'm coming to meet you. Please, come closer," Tiny said as she crawled toward them.

By morning, Tiny Snail reached the clump of dandelions. "Thank you, Dandelions, for coming to meet me," Tiny said.

Someone giggled. "The Dandelions say, 'You're welcome.'" It was Little Ant. "Crawl under," he said. "It's cool and safe." Little Ant lifted a dandelion. He was so strong.

"Thank you, Little Ant!"

"You're welcome, Tiny Snail," said the ant as he pranced away.

Tiny slept all day under the dandelions where she was cool and safe from the sun. When evening arrived, Tiny woke up. She crawled out of her hiding place. Farther up the hill, she spotted a large rock.

"Oh, Mr. Rock," she said. "I'm coming to meet you. Please, come closer."

Tiny crawled all night. Finally, Tiny Snail poked her tentacles above a tuft of grass. There was the rock.

Tiny climbed onto the rock for a better view.

"Get down!" came a gruff voice.

"Who said that?" Tiny quivered inside her shell.

"I did," said Lizard. "You're on my rock. Get down!"

Tiny scooted down as Lizard climbed up.

"Thank you, Mr. Rock, for coming to meet me." Tiny hesitated. "And thank you, Lizard, for reminding me it's time for bed."

Lizard stuck his nose high in the air. "That's 'Lazy Lizard' to you."

Tiny squirmed into a big crack in the rock and fell asleep. She slept all day in the rock's shadow where she was cool and safe from the sun.

When evening arrived, Tiny exclaimed, "Tonight I will make it to the top of the hill!"

She crawled faster and farther than she had ever crawled before. The stars still twinkled when Tiny Snail fell asleep.

When she woke up, Tiny was on a patch of dirt. The sun was high in the sky. Her skin was drying out!

"Help!" she cried. "Mr. Squirrel! Miss Butterfly! Mother Turtle, help!" But they did not hear her.

Tiny tried to hide inside her shell. It was so hot! Then a shadow fell over her. Tiny peeped out. A cloud covered the sun.

"Thank you, Cloud!" cried Tiny Snail. "Please, Clouds, clump together and block out the sun."

And they did! But it started to rain. It rained and rained until 'Whoosh!' Tiny Snail slipped backwards.

"Mud slide!" she exclaimed.

Tiny grabbed a blade of grass with her mouth and held on. The mud tried to drag her down the hill.

"Please, roots," she thought, "hold tight."

Finally, the rain stopped.

"Thank you, Grass," she said, "your roots are strong."

The Maple Tree was so close!

"Maple Tree, I'm coming to meet you. Please, come closer and be my new home."

Tiny closed her eyes and crawled with all her might.

Her tentacles bumped into something hard.

"Ouch!" she exclaimed.

Tiny opened her eyes. It was the Maple Tree!

"I'm at the top of the hill!" Tiny wiggled with glee. "Thank you, Maple Tree, for coming to meet me."

But as dawn approached, Tiny Snail frowned. Something was missing.

"You made it!" It was Mr. Squirrel.

"We're so proud of you," said Miss Butterfly.

Mother Turtle walked out of the grass. "Welcome to your new home," she said.

"Thank you, Mr. Squirrel, for urging me to try. Thank you, Miss Butterfly, for telling me to ask. And thank you, Mother Turtle, for teaching me to do a little at a time."

"There's someone you forgot to thank," said Mother Turtle.

Tiny Snail paused.

"Of course!" Her eyes glistened with delight as they bobbed on the end of her tentacles. "Me!"

SNAILS

Snails are related to squids, slugs and octopuses because they are **mollusks**. Mollusks are organized into several classes. The largest class is *Gastropoda* with more than 65,000 species of snails and slugs. The majority of these species live in the water. About one-third are land snails. Every mollusk has a soft, undivided body with no inner skeleton, and most mollusks have hard shells.

What kind of snail is Tiny?

Tiny is a land snail. Land snails are **nocturnal**. They hide in shady places during the day and feed mostly at night. They can live as long as five to eight years.

Do all snails look like Tiny?

No. Land snails have **eyes** on the end of their **tentacles**, but Tiny is the only land snail with big eyes. Her large eyes allow her to see to the top of the hill. Other land snails have tiny eyes with poor vision, so they have a second pair of tentacles called **'feelers'** which are used to smell and feel.

How does Tiny move?

Land snails move by oozing a stream of slime from a gland at the front of their **foot**. The foot is the part of the snail's body that is pushed out of the shell. The slime allows snails to slide easily over the ground.

How does Tiny drink?

Snails drink water through their skin. This is why snails prefer warm, rainy weather. When the snail's body comes in contact with moisture, the mucus on their skin absorbs the water.

How does Tiny eat?

Land snails eat broad-leafed plants and vegetables. Snails need calcium to make their shells. They get calcium by nibbling on stones, cement and soil. The **mantle**, a layer of cells that hold the **shell** to the snail's **body**, absorbs the calcium and uses it to add another layer to the shell called a **growth ring**.

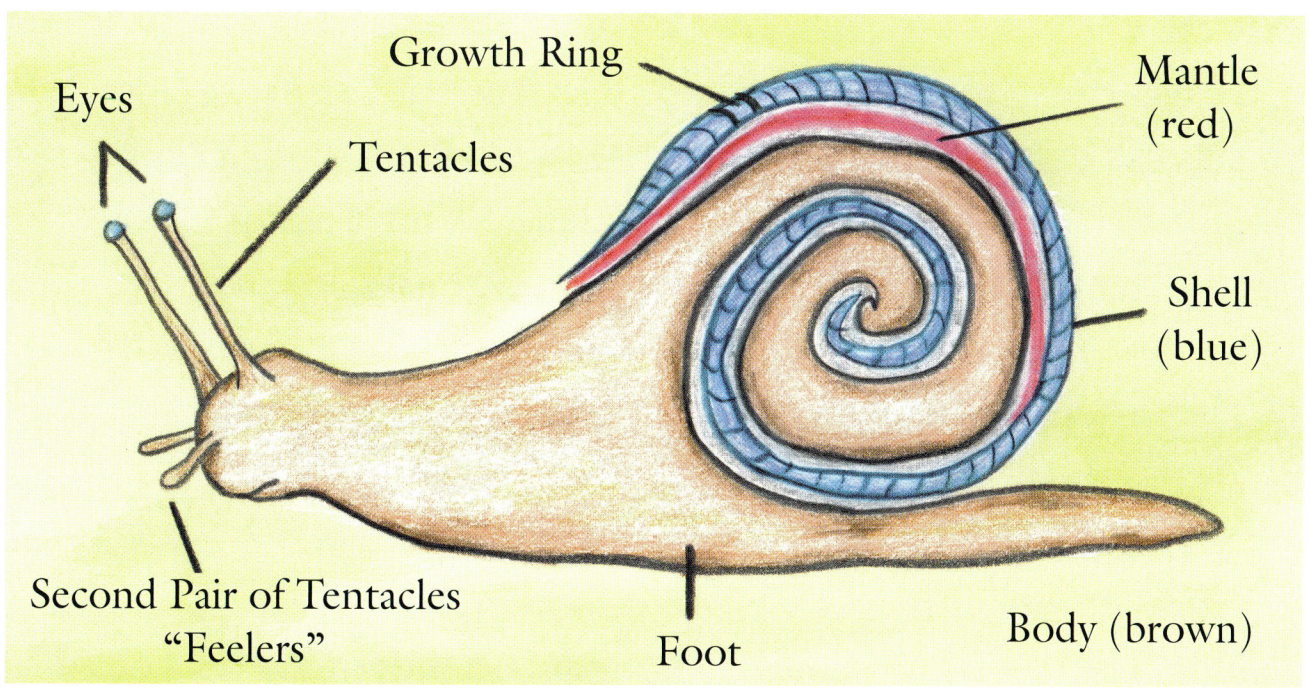

What is the difference between a land snail and a water snail?

Most land snails have two pairs of tentacles with eyes on the tips of their large tentacles. Water snails usually have one pair of tentacles, and their eyes are at the tentacles' base. Land snails breathe with lungs, while most water snails breathe with gills.

What is the largest snail?

The largest water snail is the Australian Trumpet conch. The largest ever found weighed 40 pounds, was 2.5 feet long, and over 3 feet around! The largest land snail is the Giant African Land Snail. Most are about five inches in length, but the largest ever found weighed 2 pounds and was 15.5 inches long.

Is Tiny Snail the smallest snail in the world?

No. The smallest known snail in the world is the *Ammonicera rota*. It measures only 0.02 inches across. Fifty of them laid end to end would equal one inch!

Does Tiny Snail have teeth?

Yes. Snails have thousands of tiny, sharp teeth arranged in rows on their tongue. This toothed-tongue is called a **radula**. The radula is used to cut and grind the snail's food.

What does Tiny do in the winter?

She will sleep all winter until spring. This is called hibernation. The leaves on Tiny's tree are starting to change color. Winter is coming, so Tiny will have to eat as much as possible before all the leaves change color and fall off the tree. Tiny must eat a lot of food so she will have enough energy stored up to make it through winter.

What do Tiny Snail and Little Ant have in common?

Ants can lift twenty times their own body weight. Snails are strong, too. Snails can lift ten times their own weight up a vertical surface. Ants use their antennae for touch and smell. Snails use their small tentacles for touch and smell.

ABOUT THE AUTHOR/ILLUSTRATOR

Tammy Carter Bronson is the author and illustrator of three picture books: *Tiny Snail, The Kaleidonotes and the Mixed-Up Orchestra,* and *Polliwog*. She lives in Fayetteville, Arkansas.

ILLUSTRATIONS are colored pencil and watercolor.

Hailey Bronson (pictured right) usually supervises Tammy's work.

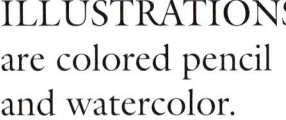

Find more **Bookaroos® Books** at www.bookaroos.com, including...

Written & Illustrated by
Tammy Carter Bronson

Polliwog emerges from the pond and learns to embrace her new life as a frog. An inspiring story that will help children overcome their fear of change. Bilingual: English and Spanish. (2004)

Library Binding
ISBN-13: 978-0-9678167-4-6 / ISBN-10: 0-9678167-4-2
Softcover
ISBN-13: 978-0-9678167-5-3 / ISBN-10: 0-9678167-5-0